The Little Yellow Car

Written and illustrated

by

Christine Penberthy

I would like to say thank you to my daughter

Louise, without her help this book would

never have been published.

xxx

The Little Yellow Car

Bert and Doris were sitting by the fire after their dinner talking about their grandchildren who had been to visit them that afternoon. They'd had such a good time kicking a football around the playing field.

Doris went to the kitchen to wash the dishes. Bert followed her into the kitchen and picked up a tea towel.

"When we have finished, I would like to go on an adventure." said Doris. "Hum" said Bert.

"Oh! Let's" said Doris. "Please, please"

"Well" said Bert "I suppose we could"

Doris ran to the front door, tossed her slippers into a corner and was putting her coat on before you could say "Jumping Jack Flash".

"I think we might need some sandwiches and bring a woolly hat too" said Bert pulling on his winter coat and tucking the big collar up under his chin.

Out in the garden they had to be very quiet. They didn't want the neighbours to hear them, this was their secret.

Slowly they pulled the doors of the garage open.

There she was, the little yellow car. Her headlights twinkled.

"Look she knows we are going on an adventure" whispered Bert

"Oh! yes," said Doris.

They didn't turn the engine on but let the little car run quietly out onto the road. The car gathered speed.

"Turn the engine on" shouted Doris.

"I will, I will" replied Bert turning the key in the ignition.

"Turn the engine on "shouted Doris again but her voice was lost in the roar that came from under the bonnet of the little yellow car. Faster and faster they went.

"Press the magic button" said Doris

Bert did press the magic button and you will never guess what happened, so I will tell you...

The little yellow car had sprouted wings.

Up, up into the dark evening skies. Past the stars, past the moon.

"Ooh, I'm a bit frightened," said Doris. Trying to hide under Bert's' big collar.

Bert was a bit frightened too, but he didn't want Doris to know.

They couldn't stop the little car once she had decided to take them on an adventure. Instead, he said

"Did you bring some sandwiches Doris?"

"Yes" said Doris coming out from under his collar "Cheese and tomato. They are here in my bag. I brought a flask of tea to".

They munched their way through the sandwiches whilst the little yellow car went on and on.

A little red light appeared ahead. Bert and Doris watched as it got bigger and bigger.

Now it was getting brighter and brighter and a spiral of stars flew across the sky.

"Ooo!" said Doris "How very beautiful".

As they got closer, they could hear something. "It sounds like music" said Doris. They drew nearer and nearer and yes it was music. Very jolly music. The kind that is played in fairgrounds.

"My goodness," said Doris. She was very excited. There, far out in space, was the most amazing fairground you have ever seen.

There were rainbow slides and real sailing boats floating on clouds.

Bumper cars that bounced and blew their horns as they tumbled about.

A beautiful pool where dolphins were giving rides, leaping over the stars above them.

The little yellow car gently touched down.

Bert and Doris stepped out into the wonderland

"I want to go on the dolphin ride it looks so exciting," said Doris.

"Be careful" said Bert looking up. It did look fun.

Doris climbed on holding very tightly to the special reins and off she went. She disappeared in an enormous spray. "Wow...." All Bert could see was the last flip of the tail as the dolphin headed higher and higher.

Up, up and over went the dolphin.

Doris could just see the stars through the spray before she headed back down to where Bert was standing.

The dolphin made a very big splash as he dived back into the water.

"It's your turn now," said Doris.

"Well" said Bert. "I really like the look of those bumper cars".

"Let's go then," said Doris.

Bert stood and looked at the bumper cars. I wonder how they find their way back.

When he got inside, he could see all the buttons were there ready to go. Bert always wanted to know how things worked.

With the door safely shut he was off. Oh! he had never had so much fun. He quite forgot where he was as he laughed and bumped and bounced about.

Every time he hit one of the little bumper cars a very loud horn went Honk! Honk! and everyone shouted hurrah!

The ride came to an end and the bumper car pulled up safely.

That was such great fun. I think I would like another go. No time he realised as he spotted Doris waving at him. He didn't want to leave her on her own any longer, he smiled and waved back.

When Bert got off Doris said "There's a little tearoom over there, shall we go and have a cup of tea? My coat is very wet from the dolphin ride, I would like to dry it out if I could".

They found a table near a radiator for Doris's coat and ordered some cakes and a pot of tea.

After cake and tea and feeling comfortable and no longer tired Bert said. "I didn't go on the rainbow slide or the sailing boats" "We could go on them now" said Doris

"We could go on them together," said Bert.

When they got to the rainbow slide Bert and Doris were very glad that they were together, because the slide was very high, and very shiny and very slippy. Bert felt Doris's hand tighten on his.

Bert was watching the faces of the people sliding down and they looked really happy and having fun. They had always been an adventurous couple, so "Come on Doris" he said and up they went.

They sat with their legs just over the edge. Doris giggled, flung her arms in the air and shouted, "Let's go".

It was spectacular. The colours of the rainbow and the flashing of the stars around them as they flew down at great speed.

At the end of the slide, there was a little soft cloud waiting for each of them. Good job too.

A little out of breath they made their way to the sailing boats.

"Look" said Bert, they are sailing on clouds.

"How amazing" said Doris." That's good I won't get wet this time.

They climbed on board and began to explore. Doris discovered two small drawers underneath the bow. She had to give it a bit of a wriggle to open it "I wonder what's inside," said Doris. She pushed her hand right to the back of one of the drawers. She pulled out a map and a book about the stars and planets.

"I wonder which planet we are on" she said.

Bert leaned over her shoulder to look but all he said was "Hum"

In the other draw they found a compass.

"This might help" he said, "now which way is north?".

"I don't think it will work up here" said Doris.

"Hum" he said. "Oh yes of course, you are right" said Bert.

"Lets see if there is anything else."

At the back of the boat, underneath the stern he found a control panel with three yellow buttons. One said 'Forward', one said 'Reverse' and the third one said 'End of the ride'. He pressed 'Forward'.

They sat on the deck and listened to the gentle swishing sound of the sails in the wind as they floated about.

"That sound reminds me," said Bert.

"What does it remind you of?" said Doris. As she looked up at him her woolly hat fell off. Bert laughed as he bent to pick it up.

"It reminds me of the holiday we had by the sea last year".

Do you know that if you hold a seashell to your ear, you can hear the waves of the sea," said Doris.

"No" said Bert "I must try that when we get home"

The sailing boat was very peaceful. The big white sails billowed out as they floated softly around and around.

Bert looked at Doris and she was fast asleep.

"Wakey, wakey" he said, "I think it's time to go home"

He leaned over and pressed the button saying 'End of the ride'.

Bert and Doris stepped off the boat into the car park of the funfair.

What a wonderful time they had had.

As they walked over towards the little yellow car, Doris saw a

drinking fountain ahead. "I am quite thirsty" she said.

"Me too" said Bert.

The water in the drinking fountain tasted so good.

"Ah!" that's better" said Bert.

The little yellow car took them home so quickly that the next thing

they knew was, with a soft little bump, they found themselves

outside their house again.

Home safe and happy together.

The End

Printed in Great Britain
by Amazon

11525372R00016